GOBLINS

GOBLINS

Written by Leslie McGuire

Illustrated by Dennis Hockerman

ISBN 1-931020-03-5   First Edition   1 2 3 4 5 6 7 8 9 10

Contents

Special Words

Special words help make this story fun.
Your child may need help reading them.

head

nose

promise

1. Something Fishy Going On

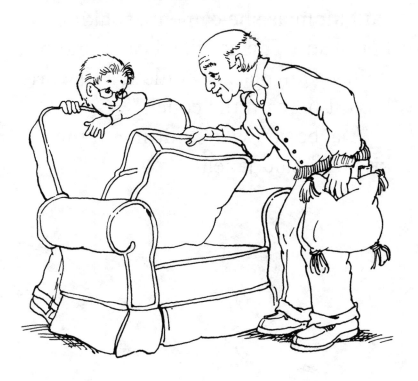

"Where did I leave my glasses?" said Grandpop. He lifted the pillows off his chair, looked, and then put them back down again.

"Let me help you look," said Sam.

"Thank you," said Grandpop. "I can't see a thing without my glasses."

"I do not know what's happening,"
said Mom as she came in, shaking
her head. "This is silly. I can't find my
knitting anyplace! I could have sworn
I left it here on the couch."

"Maybe you were knitting in the
kitchen," said Janet.

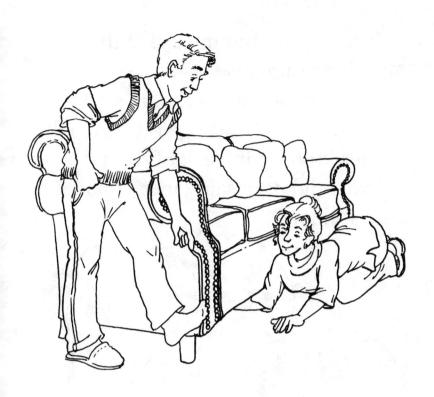

"I never knit in the kitchen," said Mom. She peeked under the couch.

That's when Dad limped in with only one slipper on.

"Did you see my other slipper?" he asked. "I know I had two of them last night. I left them under the bed. Now I can find only one!"

"I could not find my jacket this morning," said Janet.

"I bet you left it at school," said Mom. She was bending down to look for her knitting in back of the TV.

"No, I did not," said Janet. "I had it on last night."

Just then Buddy the dog came into the room. He was running his nose around the base of the walls, snorting and sniffing in the corners.

"Looks to me as if he's lost a bone," said Grandpop. "At least we are not the only ones who can't find things."

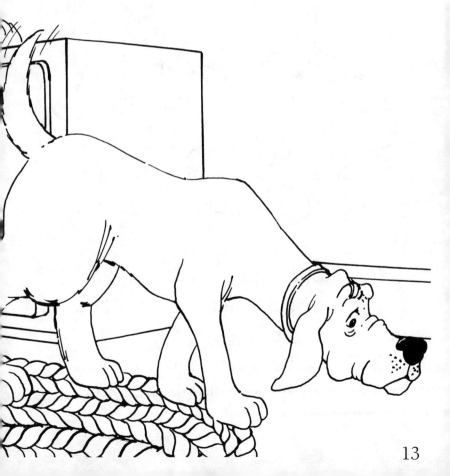

"His bone is not lost," said Janet.
"He just forgot where he put it! He
does that all of the time."

Buddy gave Janet a gloomy look
and sniffed his way back out the door.

Janet shook her head, saying, "This is very odd."

"Oh boy," said Grandpop. "No one can find anything in this house."

That's when Sam said, "By the way, did you take my toy train? It's missing."

"What would I do with a toy train?"
asked Grandpop.

"You like my train," said Sam.

"I like your train," said Grandpop,
"but I am too old to play with trains."

"This is getting silly," said Mom, going back into the kitchen. "Maybe if we all stop looking for things, we'll all start finding them."

"Who knows?" said Sam, cheerfully. "Maybe all of our stuff will turn up in the morning."

"I hope so," said Dad as he limped slowly upstairs.

Sam was now by himself in the living room. He plopped himself down on the couch and started to think.

"There's something fishy going on here," he said to himself. "If you ask me, it looks as if someone or something is taking things. But who, or what, could it be?"

Buddy came back in, grunted, and flopped his head down on Sam's leg.

"Are you taking our stuff, Buddy?" Sam asked.

Buddy showed Sam the whites of his eyes and groaned a sad dog groan.

"I am sorry, Buddy," Sam said, patting his dog on the nose. "I know you would never do such a thing. But who would?"

Buddy opened his eyes and started to growl.

"Do you know who is doing this?" Sam asked, looking at Buddy.

Buddy wagged his tail and snarled, but he would not get up.

"He knows something," Sam said to himself.

2. Midnight in the Kitchen

Late that night, Sam was sleeping in his bed when he felt a cold wet thing on his cheek. He jumped. His eyes shot open.

"Who? What? Where?" he said in a sleepy voice. "Oh. It's just you Buddy. Go to sleep."

But Buddy would not go away.
He grabbed Sam's pajama leg and
yanked. He was trying to tug him
out of bed.

"Go away, Buddy," Sam muttered.
But Buddy just pulled harder.

"What do you want?" Sam
snapped. But getting angry woke him
up. That's when he knew that Buddy
was trying to tell him something.

Buddy put his nose down and started to creep out of the room with his belly on the floor. Sam grabbed his glasses and a flashlight and was right with him.

"What is it? What did you see, Buddy?" he whispered.

Buddy just turned his head and frowned at Sam as if to say, "Hush up!"

Sam stayed right in back of Buddy as they inched their way down the hall and down the stairs. Then Buddy stopped short. Sam bumped into him. They peeked into the kitchen.

The light from the full moon streamed in the windows. Everything in the kitchen looked as if it had been dusted with silver.

Just then an odd little blob with stubby arms and legs shot across the kitchen floor. It hopped onto the countertop. Sam clapped his hand over his mouth. Buddy's fur was standing on end.

The blob was dragging a little sack. It lifted the lid of the candy jar and started to stuff candy into the sack!

All of a sudden, another little blob
hopped onto the windowsill. It
grabbed the stuffed sack and ran off.
Sam could not stand it anymore.

"Give that candy back!" he yelled.

The little blob slowly turned and
looked right at him.

For the first time, Sam could see
a little, wrinkly face with a big nose
and little black eyes.

But before he could say anything,
it vanished.

"Get him!" he hissed to Buddy.
The two of them ran out into the
back yard.

The moon made all of the trees and shrubs look like silver. The only sound was the chirping of crickets. Buddy shot off into the garden, his nose tracking all of the way.

28

First he went left. Then he went right. Then he backtracked. Then he stopped by the peach tree. Sam could see he had lost the smell.

"Whatever they are, they got away with our candy," he whispered.

All of a sudden, Buddy froze and started to whine.

Sam rushed over to him. He was stuck in one spot!

Sam reached out his hand.

He was about to grab Buddy when there was a very odd tingly feeling in his legs. The tingly feeling got stronger and stronger. Soon Sam's arms started to feel tingly. Then his face felt really tingly. He felt himself slipping on the grass as things around him seemed to get bigger and bigger.

"What's happening?" he started to ask Buddy.

Then everything went black.

3. Six Hundred Years of Mistakes

Sam woke up with a pain in his ears.

Slowly he opened his eyes. He was in a funny brown room. There were tree roots hanging down from the dirt walls. All around him were odd little people with little wrinkly faces, big noses, and shiny black eyes.

Each one wore a pointed hat that was battered and patched. Their shirts and pants were old and grubby. They wore big shoes with long pointy toes that curled up in the air.

They did not look happy.

"It's about time," said one. "We have been waiting for you!"

Sam found his voice and said, "Who are you?"

"We are your garden goblins," said the fat one. "My name is Ork. I know that your name is Sam, and your big hairy thing up there is called Buddy."

"How did I get here?" asked Sam. "Did you guys get bigger?"

"No, you got smaller," said Ork. "We shrank you."

"That's right," said the tall one. "My name is Borg, and you are in our cave under the peach tree."

"What do you want?" asked Sam.

"It is clear to us that people no longer know how to treat their garden goblins," said Ork. "For starters, you never put out milk and crackers for us. You should do that every night. If you do that, we will not upset your cows and goats. We will not knock down your fences or steal your chickens!"

"But we do not have cows, goats, fences, or chickens," said Sam.

"So what?" said Borg. "It's the same thing. Whatever you have, we will not snatch or break it."

Sam did not say anything for a while. It was hard to think.

"I did not know there was such a thing as goblins," said Sam. "But I am very sorry that I did not do the right thing. I will put out milk and crackers every night from now on."

Ork looked very pleased at this.

"Goblins have been here under this peach tree for six hundred years," said Borg. "The very first goblins came here on big ships from the Land of Never-Ending Snow."

"They hid in sacks of dry fish in the bottom of the ships," said Ork.

"It smelled very bad. It took a long time, but we are glad they came.

"Now we want people to know we are here. They forgot about goblins. Six hundred years is too long for a proper goblin to go without being treated to gifts of milk and crackers."

"Did you take the knitting and my train and all of that stuff?" asked Sam.

"We do not take things," said Borg, looking very grumpy. "We like to think of it as a loan."

"You mean, you will give it all back?" Sam asked.

"When we are finished with it, yes," said Ork. "Now, would you like to see our town?"

4. The Full Moon

Sam went with Ork and Borg. They
said the underground town had been
a rabbit nest in the old days. The
goblins had made it much bigger over
the years. They went down long tubes
that led to bigger and bigger rooms.

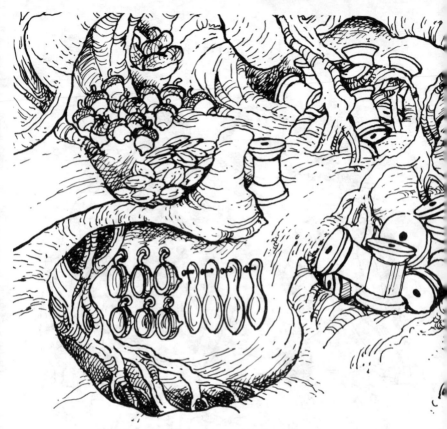

Some rooms were filled with nuts, others with grass. Seed pods to make cups and spoons were stacked to the top in one room. One room was filled with empty spools. These made good seats for goblins.

"Hey!" Sam said outside one of the rooms. "Is that my toy train?"

"Yes," said Borg, "but we do not know what it's for. Can you tell us?"

Sam did not know if he wanted to tell him. After all, it was his train!

"It does not do much," said Sam. "You have to push it around on tracks."

"Then you will make the tracks for us," said Ork.

After what felt like miles, they came to a really big room. There were wooden planks and spool chairs set up everywhere. A firefly lamp was in every corner. The lamps lit the room with a soft, flickering light. A grasshopper band was setting up in a corner.

"This is where we have a big party whenever there is a full moon," said Ork. "We make sure there is an elf for every goblin to dance with. We also ask the Fairy King to come."

"You are lucky because the party will start very soon," said Borg.

"But I do not know how to dance," said Sam. "Besides, I should go home soon. It's late."

"Too late to back out now!" sang Ork. "Here they come!"

The next thing Sam knew, the room was filled with the oddest little people he had ever seen. Some had wings. Some wore leaf outfits or cobweb dresses. Some walked, some ran, and some flew. Some had green skin and silver hair.

He drank something yummy from a seed pod. He ate cakes made from sweet nuts.

The grasshopper band was really neat, and Sam joined the long line of dancing, jumping, hopping, flapping little people. It was a very merry party—the best he had ever seen.

It felt as if no time had passed when the last dancer left the room. Sam rubbed his eyes. He was starting to feel sleepy.

Ork looked at him and said, "Look at that. This small one is up past his bedtime. He is, after all, not a goblin."

"We should take him back to his garden and his big, hairy critter," said Borg.

With one goblin on each side, they helped Sam back along all of the tubes until they were back in the first room.

"Before you go back, we want three things from you," said Borg.

"First, we want you to promise that you will not forget to put out milk and crackers every night," said Borg. "The next thing we want is for you to promise that you will come back to our full moon party whenever you can."

"I can do that—and the milk and crackers," said Sam in a sleepy voice.

"The third thing is this," said Ork, getting Sam's hand. "We want you to have this gift and keep it with you always. That way you will not forget that goblins are real."

Sam looked down and saw a small, green ball with a light deep inside of it.

5. A Goblin Gift

In a flash, Sam found himself sitting
on the grass in his back yard. Buddy
was still standing right where Sam
had left him. He was still stuck and
could have been made of stone. Sam
scratched his ears, and all of a sudden
Buddy jumped. He started to lick Sam's
face and hands.

"Good boy!" said Sam.

That's when Sam opened his fist
and saw the shimmering green ball.

"Maybe it's magic," he said
to himself.

"That ball has more magic in it
than anything you have ever seen,"
came a voice from the top of the
peach tree.

"Who's there?" asked Sam,
looking up. He did not see anyone,
but someone was talking to him.

"I do not think we have met," said
the voice. Then Sam could hear the
sound of wings.

"I am the Mighty Owl, thank you very much," said a barn owl as it landed on his head. "You go to bed before I get up."

"I did not know that owls could talk," said Sam.

"How silly," said the owl. "All of us can talk. It's just that people cannot understand us."

"How come I can understand you now?" asked Sam. He had the feeling that the owl did not think he was very smart.

"You can understand me now
because of the magic green ball," said
the owl. "You can understand what
everyone has to say."

"Everyone?" asked Sam.

Just then, Buddy rubbed his leg and
said, "Yep, even dogs!"

"You have got to be kidding!" said
Sam. "Dogs can't talk!"

"Oh, yes they can," said the owl. "You just can't understand them."

"That ball is the best gift anyone could possibly get," said Buddy. "You are a very lucky boy—and not just because you have me as a pet!"

"Did you always know what I was saying?" asked Sam.

"I did," said Buddy.

"So how come you always acted as if you did not understand any of it?" asked Sam.

"Too many chores," said Buddy. "Fetch this! Sit down! Get off the couch! Go here! Go there! Life is better when you are just a dog."

"That's right," said the owl.

"It's getting light," said Buddy.
"Time to go back inside and get into
bed. That way, Mom and Dad will
not know that you have been out
all night."

"Oh, my gosh!" said Sam. "We had
better hurry!"

"I trust I will see you two again,"
said the owl, waving a wing at them
as they dashed to the house.

Sam and Buddy got as far as the porch. There was Mom, and she looked mad.

"What are you doing out in the night?" she asked.

"Um," said Sam.

"Just say you took me out for a walk. I was scratching to be let out," Buddy whispered.

"Oh, forget it," said Mom. "Just come inside and go right back to bed."

"Thank you," said Sam as they went upstairs.

"No problem," said Buddy.

"I think that this magic is going to be really good," said Sam. "I can help you, and you can help me."

"I know," said Buddy. "It will be so nice to talk with someone. Dogs can get lonely sometimes, too."

And so, every night after that, Sam
set out a glass of milk and a plate
of crackers. Whenever the moon was
full, he and Buddy waited under the
peach tree for the full moon party
to start.

Sam made train tracks for the
goblins and had a much better
time with his train than he had
ever had before.

The owl was the best teacher
Sam had ever had, and Buddy was
the best pal any boy could wish for.